This book
belongs to:

_____

MESSAGE TO PARENTS

This book is perfect for parents and children to read aloud together. First read the story to your child. When you read it again run your finger under each line, stopping at each picture for your child to "read." Help your child to figure out the picture. If your child makes a mistake, be encouraging as you say the right word. Point out the written word beneath each picture in the margin on the page. Soon your child will be "reading" aloud with you, and at the same time learning the symbols that stand for words.

EDITED BY
DEBORAH SHINE

DESIGN BY
CANARD DESIGN, INC.

Henny Penny

A Read Along With Me Book

Retold by Joan Powers

Illustrated by Jill Dubin

CHECKERBOARD PRESS
NEW YORK

Henny
Penny

woods

acorn

tree

King

One day was walking in

the when suddenly – whack!

– a big fell from a and

hit her on the head.

"Goodness me!" said .

"The sky is falling. I must go and

tell the  ."

So started on her way.

Very soon she met .

"Cock-a-doodle-doo!" said

 . "Where are you going this

fine day?"

"Oh, my," said . "The sky is

falling and I am off to tell the ."

Cocky
Locky

**Cocky
Locky**

**Henny
Penny**

two

King

**Ducky
Lucky**

"Cock-a-doodle-doo, is that

so?" said . "May I come

with you?"

"Certainly," said . "The **2**

of us will go and tell the ." So

they went on their way, and before

long they met .

"Quack, quack. Where are you going?" asked .

"We're going to tell the 🐶 the sky is falling," said 🐓.

"May I come with you to tell the 🐶?" asked 🦢.

Henny
Penny

Cocky
Locky

three

King

Ducky
Lucky

"Certainly," said and .

"The of us will go and tell the

." So , , and

went to tell the the sky was

falling.

Along the way they met .

"Honk, honk," said .

"Where are you going this fine

day?"

"We are going to tell the

the sky is falling," said .

King

Goosey
Loosey

3
three

4
four

"May I come with you to tell the ?" asked .

"Certainly," said the **3** friends.

"The **4** of us will go and tell the the sky is falling."

So on their way went the 4

friends, and a little piece down

the road they met .

"Gobble, gobble," said .

"Where are you going this fine

day?"

Turkey
Lurkey

King

Henny
Penny

woods

Goosey
Loosey

Turkey
Lurkey

"Oh, we are going to tell the

the sky is falling. A piece of it fell

on 's head when she was

walking in the ," said  .

"Gobble, gobble, is that so?"

said  . "May I come along

with you?"

"Certainly," they all said together. "The **5** of us will go and tell the ."

They went on their way and soon met .

five

Foxy Loxy

Foxy
Loxy

Turkey
Lurkey

Henny
Penny

woods

5
five

King

"Good morning, my friends,"

said . "Where are you going

this very fine day?"

"Oh, my," said . " was

in the  when a piece of the

sky fell on her head. So the

of us are off to tell the the

sky is falling."

"What terrible news," said .

"I'll show you the way to the .

Just follow me."

So the **5** friends followed

and soon they came to a hole in

the ground. "This is a shortcut to

the ," said , licking his lips.

Foxy
Loxy

King

5

five

It was really the entrance to 's lair. "I will go in first. Each of you must follow me. Then we will find the ."

"These **5** friends will make a good dinner," thought to himself.

and all her friends promised

to follow . and her

friends walked toward the hole.

Then she suddenly remembered

something.

"Oh, my," she said. "I forgot to

lay an today. You must all

go tell the without me." And

off she went down the road.

 , ,  , and

watched her go.

Henny
Penny

egg

Cocky
Locky

Ducky
Lucky

Goosey
Loosey

Turkey
Lurkey

Foxy Loxy

palace

Goosey Loosey

King

" knows the way to the ," said . "Let him tell the  the sky is falling. I have work to do." "We do, too," said the others, and they all hurried away.

sat in his lair and waited for

 and her friends. He was very

hungry. Finally he came out of

the hole and looked around.

 , , , and  had all gone home!

And so went without his

dinner, and no one ever told the

 the sky was falling.

Henny
Penny

Cocky
Locky

Ducky
Lucky

Turkey
Lurkey